Alex Flors

MAD ENOUGH TO LOVE YOU

—

DESIRE

Mad Enough to Love You: Desire

DISCLAIMER: This is a work of fiction. Names, characters, events, and places are either the product of the author's imagination or used fictitiously. Any resemblance to actual persons, living or dead, or actual events is purely coincidental.

ISBN: 978-0-9926555-6-3 (eBook)
ISBN: 978-0-9926555-7-0 (Paperback)

Alex Florschutz
Forest Row, UK
Ubud, Bali
www.florschutz.com

For the ones who knew better
but did it anyway.

"First the flood, then the green, then the gold.
All things ripen. All things fall."

TABLE OF CONTENTS

Prologue

BEFORE WE BEGAN

"And once the storm is over, you won't remember how you made it through... But one thing is certain. When you come out of the storm, you won't be the same person who walked in."

— **Haruki Murakami**

There was a moment before him, before any of it, when I stood alone in the fields, watching the land breathe.

The rice had just been cut. The stubs stood raw and broken, the scent of damp earth rising thick into the evening air. Smoke curled from a distant pile of husks, its slow spiral vanishing into the gold-streaked sky.

I had been in Bali long enough to understand its rhythm.

First, the flood. Water pooling in the paddies, drowning the past to make way for what comes next.

Then, the green. The slow, steady rise, unseen until one day, it is undeniable.

Then, the gold. The tipping point, the moment before the cut. The moment before everything is lost to begin again.

I knew this. Had watched it happen over and over. But I had

never felt it move through me. Not like this.

Not until him.

Even then, before I knew his name, before his hands had mapped my body, before his voice had settled into the places I did not know were waiting for him, I felt it coming.

A shift in the air. A pressure in my bones. Something stirring beneath the surface, restless and waiting.

The inevitable.

I should have known, but desire moves like seasons. Long before we notice, the change is already in motion. And once it begins, there is no stopping the flood.

Chapter 1

THE LOOK THAT STARTED IT ALL

"Love does not grow where it is told,
but where it chooses."
— Old Proverb

It was nothing.

Just a fleeting glance.

Barely anything at all. Or at least that's what I told myself.

He was filming the land ceremony for me, the one asking the gods' permission to allow the rice field to accommodate my villa. I sat cross-legged on the dry stubble of the recent harvest, my kebaya and sarong soft against my skin, while the priest's bell rang with devotion and incense coiled around me, dense and sweet.

The setting sun painted gold over everything. That impossible Bali light, molten and holy, like it knew all your secrets. I thought of the first time the island worked its strange magic on me. And of how magic here often comes with a cost.

The Balinese women moved in practiced choreography, flicking water in wide arcs, and scattered petals like whispered prayers. Children fed the small fire with handfuls of dry grass. The mangku chanted, his voice drifting into the twilight, asking the unseen to bless the work ahead.

A sudden gust of wind disrupted the stillness like a strange omen. Maybe the gods saw it first before either of us knew what lay ahead. Like they had glimpsed the fault lines that shifted quietly beneath the surface, waiting for the inevitable crack.

And yet everything felt untouched. Ordinary. As if nothing had shifted.

But it had.

Beyond the paddies, the earth lay turned and waiting. The ducks had done their work, feet churned the mud, beaks snapped up what was left behind. Water pooled in the furrows, catching the last of the light. Soon, the shoots would come. Then green. Then gold. Then, the cut. The cycle ticking forward whether we noticed or not.

He looked up from behind the camera. His eyes found mine. Dark. Searching. Almost amused. And in that brief collision, something took root. A question neither of us voiced. A charge so sudden and sharp I forgot how to breathe.

Then, the moment passed. He looked away. I turned back to the ceremony, to the priest, and to the work still ahead. The foundation to pour. The walls to build. Sketches of the villa waiting on my desk back in Ubud. Pages of ideas scribbled in charcoal and ink. I had been painting it in my mind for months, laying colour over outlines, imagining how light would spill across the floors, how shadows would stretch in the afternoons. How the rice would move through its seasons. And I could paint that too.

I'd been here before. Different man. Different lifetime. I knew better.

But desire does not care about what you know. It grows anyway.

Like rice. First, the flood. Then, the slow, steady rise. Until it is too late to stop the harvest.

Chapter 2

QUEEN OF DENIAL

"Desire is like the tide,
it comes whether we call it or not."
— **Unknown**

I returned to Bali to build a quiet life. Steady. Safe. A sanctuary of my own design after years of chaos and heartbreak.

I was not here for love. God, no. I had done that already. I knew how it would end. I was the original gangster of following my passion. Please. I could have written the manual.

Until he arrived.

A rough-edged Balinese contractor with forearms like rope and that impossible mix of charm and danger. Black hair, slicked back from the heat. A grin that could undo a lifetime of self-discipline.

He had worked on cruise ships around the world, so his English was good, his understanding of my world sufficient. And yet, he belonged to this island in a way I never could. I was a bulé, always passing through, no matter how long I stayed. The land might let me borrow its beauty, but it would never claim me as its own. He moved like he was part of it. As if the earth itself bent slightly to greet him.

Younger. Cocky. Off-limits.

Not that I cared.

He always met me with a broad smile, a firm handshake, palm to chest, and a respectful head bow. His business partner was his opposite, gentle, reliable, safely unremarkable.

But this man.

This man I could not stop watching.

I cannot remember when it started. The flirting, that is.

Maybe it was not even flirting at first. Just long conversations that drifted past work and into something more intimate. He shared stories of travel, of unrequited love, of a rebound marriage. I shared my tangled history of what it meant to love and lose on this island.

Then, out of nowhere, he started saying things like:

"Where have you been? I have missed you," with that grin, the kind that tests the water but already knows it's warm.

Why did he say that?

At first, I told myself it was harmless. Just playful banter. A bit of good-natured teasing to break up the workday.

But chemistry is not reasonable.

It just reacts.

You cannot stop a storm by telling it no.

It started with glances. Then, accidental touches. Private jokes. Lingering moments where neither of us moved away fast enough. I rolled my eyes at his ridiculous comments, pretending I had not noticed the slow burn creeping across my skin.

It made no sense. And yet, I wanted him.

There I was, a respectable woman in her fifties, admired and accomplished, pretending I was not unravelling every time he looked at me like I was a secret he was ready to risk.

And him?

He never once pretended otherwise.

Together, we were an unholy adventure waiting to happen.

Chapter 3

PLAYING WITH FIRE

"Some loves are not meant to last.
They are meant to set you on fire."
— **Beau Taplin**

It was dangerous, this thing between us.

Not just because of the age difference. Or the fact that I was his boss. Or even that his wife waited at home, her world separate but tethered to his.

It was dangerous because I wanted it.

I should have known better. And yet, knowing had never stopped me before.

We worked side by side every day. He oversaw the builders, the materials, the movement of earth and stone that would eventually become my home. I oversaw him. Or at least, I tried to.

Some things slip through unnoticed.

But some things you let slip through.

I started to notice the way his shirt clung to his back when he wiped the sweat from his brow. The way his hands lingered just a second too long when he passed me a receipt. The way his voice dropped to something quieter, something for me alone when the others could not hear.

I should have ended it then.

Should have drawn a line.

Should have made it clear.

But instead, I let it build.

A game neither of us acknowledged, but both of us played.

One afternoon, I leaned against the edge of an unfinished wall, watching the men haul bricks and mix cement. The air was thick with dust and heat. He stood next to me, close enough that his thigh nearly brushed mine.

He nudged me with his elbow. "You look beautiful today," he said, his gaze drifting over my outfit. His body shone, bronze and burnished beneath the sun.

"Thank you," I scoffed a little too quickly. The compliment settled in my chest, warm yet unwelcome.

"I miss you when you don't visit," he teased, leaning back on a pile of tiles, arms crossed, with that grin. "Why don't you visit more?"

The way he looked at me left no room for doubt. I swear the space between us felt charged, as though his hands were already on me. I sat down beside him before I could think better of it, his presence enveloping me like an invisible cloak.

"Oh, you know. Too much fun to have elsewhere," I said, trying to keep it light.

"Why don't you have fun with me?"

Something in my stomach flipped, my body answering before my mind could intervene. I forced a laugh, turned back to the view, but I could feel his eyes on me.

Assessing. Waiting.

I should have stood up then.

Should have walked away.

Instead, I let the moment settle between us, thick and unspoken.

The men worked on around us, oblivious or pretending to be. Part of me wondered how they could not see it. The pull. Pheromones stirring from hibernation. The base of my spine tingled.

Don't go there, I told myself. Do not fall for his charm. Was this how he treated all his clients?

I swallowed hard, forcing my voice to be steady but still friendly. "Get back to work."

His smile never faltered. "Yes, boss."

At lunch, I caught him watching me. Not staring. Observing, quietly, as if he committed me to memory, in that way no one else had in years. I looked down at my phone to check messages, though nothing waited for me.

"Careful, Queen," he said later as I navigated a narrow walkway. "Wouldn't want you falling for me."

I rolled my eyes, but my smile betrayed me. "You are impossible."

"And yet, here you are. Still hiring me. Still talking to me. Still looking at me like that."

"Like what?"

He shrugged, brushed past me, his arm grazing mine just enough to short-circuit whatever thought I was holding.

"You know."

And I did.

The afternoons stretched longer, slow as the water pausing in the paddies. My visits to the site grew like the first green shoots, quietly multiplying without notice. The touches lingered. The conversations wandered. The rice fields beyond shifted from water to green shoots. Time slipping, seasons changing, the inevitable harvest appearing faint on the horizon.

Every part of me knew this was foolish. Every part of me wanted more. The danger was part of the wanting, like standing at the edge of something vast, knowing one more step would tip me into the unknown, and craving the fall anyway.

Chapter 4

THE SPACE BETWEEN US

"There are two kinds of secrets: those we keep from others and those we hide from ourselves."
— **Frank Warren**

There is a moment before something becomes real. A moment when you could still walk away, still pretend you do not want it, still tell yourself the ground beneath you has not already shifted.

I lived in that moment for weeks.

Balanced on the edge. One foot in, one foot out.

I told myself I was imagining things. That the way he looked at me, longer than necessary, deeper than appropriate, was nothing. That the way he always seemed to find me in the worksite full of men was coincidence. That the space between us was not charged. That I was not waiting for something I had no business waiting for.

But we knew.

And knowing changes everything.

It was dusk when he finally said something real.

We stood together overlooking the land, waterlogged paddies giving way to green, shadows creeping in. The air was still. Potent.

The sweat on my back slid slow as honey. The insect choir rose with the fading light.

The workers had gone home, leaving behind the scent of damp earth and clove smoke.

"It's getting there," he said, nodding to the emerging buildings.

I smiled. "Yes."

A pause. A breath.

His gaze moved across my face. Slow. Searching.

"And then what?" he asked.

I turned to him, brows raised. "What do you mean?"

He exhaled, shaking his head, a half-smile curving his lips. "You know what I mean."

And I did.

Because the moment the villa was complete, there would be no more excuses.

No more daily meetings.

No more casual conversations stolen between measurements and cement pours.

No more reasons to see each other.

I sighed and looked back at the horizon as if the answer was somewhere in the fields. "I suppose we go back to our lives."

His voice was quiet but sure. "You think that is possible?"

I did not answer.

The truth hung between us, unspoken.

It was full of things unsaid.

And silence had never felt so loud.

"Before you," he said quietly, "I felt nothing."

I turned to him. His face was unreadable, carved in twilight, but something in his voice had softened.

"And now?" I asked.

He tilted his head, weighing the risk. "And now I wonder."

"Wondering what?"

"If you are as dangerous as you look."

I laughed, but the sound felt foreign. Like an attempt to fill the space with something lighter than the truth.

My heart had already leapt.

"Only if you are mad enough to find out."

He smiled then. Slow. Devastating.

"Oh, I am mad enough."

A breeze tugged at the hem of my dress. Barely a whisper against my skin. It felt good.

I thought of the offerings left at the shrine that morning. Coloured petals, delicate and unfolding. Incense curling into the ether.

Just like us, maybe. Beautiful. Fragile. Profound.

Destined to collapse under the weight of its own desire.

A quiet warning.

Some things are not meant to last. Beauty like this slips through your fingers while you try to hold on.

As if the gods had turned their backs.

Or worse.

They were watching.

Waiting.

Chapter 5

JUST ONE MORE MOMENT

"The heart has its reasons which reason knows nothing of."
— **Blaise Pascal**

The next time I saw him, it was raining.

Not the usual tropical downpour, but softer. Mistier. The kind of rain that clung to skin and hair, beads on lips like they waited to be tasted.

I came to check on the progress. That was the excuse.

The foundations were already in place, two men had dug the pool by hand.

But when I arrived, the crew had gone for lunch.

Only him, alone, dragging on a cigarette in the unfinished space, music playing low from his phone.

He glanced up, surprised, but then that slow smile spread across his face as if he had been standing by.

And suddenly, I felt the ground tilt, the space between us corrupted with the weight of the inevitable.

"Queen," he said, as if the word belonged to me. "You are late."

"Better late than never," I said, shaking the rain from my hair.

He watched me do it. Watched the droplets slide down my arms.

And I watched him watching me.

For a while, we pretended to care about pool tiles.

He pointed at colour samples. I nodded.

We stood shoulder to shoulder, tension coiling around us, and neither of us moved.

His sleeve brushed my bare arm and sent a quiet pulse through the space we had not yet crossed.

And then, somehow, his hand was at the small of my back, guiding me beneath the tarpaulin.

"You should stay out of the rain," he murmured, voice low and rough.

"It is only water."

"Still."

His hand lingered.

His thumb brushed the fabric of my dress in the faintest, most accidental way.

But it was not an accident.

We both knew.

I turned to face him, meaning to say something clever. Something polite. Something to stop what was already evolving.

But the words never came.

Because he looked at me like I was the answer to something he had not even known he was asking.

"This is dangerous," I whispered.

He nodded. "I know."

Neither of us moved.

The rain outside thickened, tapping against the tarp like a heartbeat.

And then, like a dare, like an inevitability, he stepped closer.

Close enough that I could smell the faint spice of his skin, his heat rising through the damp air.

"I think about you," he said, barely above a whisper. "More than I should."

It was not smooth. It was not rehearsed.

It was raw like the words surprised him as much as they did me.

And there, right there, was the point where I could have laughed it off.

Could have reminded him I was his client.

Could have gathered my things, walked out, and let the rain swallow me whole.

Instead, I said, "Me too."

The moment snapped tight between us, stretched thin as I trembled.

His breath, shallow and fast.

My pulse, quick and light.

Tension gathered low. Deep. As if every part of me was braced for the fall.

He leaned in. Not enough to kiss me. Just enough for our foreheads to nearly touch.

"Tell me to stop," he said.

But I did not.

I could not.

Not now.

So we stood there. Not kissing. Not touching.

But somehow closer than skin.

Just one more moment.

And then another.

And another.

Until there was no such thing as stopping.

Until voices stirred in the distance, footsteps crunched on gravel. The builders returning from lunch.

And still, neither of us moved.

Chapter 6

THE EDGE OF IT

"We do not choose whom we love.
We only choose how much it destroys us."
— **Unknown**

After that night, everything shifted.

Nothing happened. Not really.

Unless you count the way my body tuned itself to the sound of his voice.

Days passed in a blur. We kept up the act.

I walked the site, nodded at walls, pointed at fixtures. Things that used to matter.

The rice was taller now. The fields had gone from water to green. That slow, steady swell towards gold. The inevitable pull of things becoming what they are meant to be.

And under it all, the current ran wild.

I felt him before I saw him. The shift in the air.

Like the space changed shape to let him in.

"You are quiet today," he said, handing me a bottle of water.

Our fingers brushed.

A spark.

A dare.

"Thinking." Though I could not have said about what.

"About me?"

Almost a joke.

Almost.

I did not answer. We both knew.

We stood together, surveying the land. The villa taking shape. Lines rising from the earth. My dream solidifying around us. And still, all I could think about was the space between our arms. How little it would take to close it. And God, I wanted to.

"You are trouble." His voice low, like a confession.

I laughed, but it caught. "I am not the one starting this."

"Aren't you?"

His eyes dropped to my mouth.

Brief.

Enough.

And just like that, the pretending was over.

This thing, whatever it was, whatever it wanted to be, was no longer subtle.

I turned to leave, but he walked me to my bike.

The air hung heavy and wet. Storm clouds piled above the paddies, dark and swollen, ready to break.

"Are you sure you want to drive in this?" he asked, standing over me like he belonged there.

"I will manage."

He nodded, watching me with that same unreadable expression.

Patience.

Hunger.

The kind of look that felt certain.

When I turned the key, he leaned in.

Close.

Breath on my cheek.

"Careful, Queen," he murmured. "These roads get slippery when wet."

I almost laughed. Rolled my eyes.

Almost.

Not a joke. Not really.

A warning.

A promise.

I pulled on my helmet and rode away.

Heart pounding.

Head scrambled.

But the way he said it, we both knew he was not talking about the rain.

Chapter 7

THE RIDE

"You only have to let the soft animal of your body love what it loves."
— **Mary Oliver**

It was supposed to be practical.

Just a trip to the big supplier in Denpasar to pick out toilets and taps and a hundred other things that needed my attention, whether I liked it or not.

But practicality vanished the moment he said, "You are not riding your bike down there."

"I have done it before," I shrugged.

"Not with me around."

And that was that.

No smile. No argument. Just quiet certainty, as if keeping me safe, was already his decision to make.

The morning he came to collect me, I heard the bike before I saw him. That low growl breaking the hush of the lane. Helmet under his arm. Hair damp from the shower. Skin still shining from the early heat.

"Ready, Queen?"

I nodded. Climbed on.

Arms around his waist.

Contact I had not prepared for. Warm. Solid. Inevitable.

It should have been just a ride.

But there is something about the back of a bike. The way you have to give in. Lean close. Trust someone else with the road ahead.

The wind pressed us together. My legs against his. My hands resting light at first, like I was still pretending this was only transport.

By the bypass, I had given up.

He caught my arms and pulled them tighter. My chest flush against his back.

And I felt him feel it.

Quiet.

Sure.

A secret tucked between us.

We did not speak much on the way down. We did not need to.

The rice fields we passed were shifting from bright green to a deeper shade. Growth happening in silence. The next stage unfolding, with or without us.

At the store, we played our parts.

Tiles. Washbasins. Paint swatches. Wood, metal, glass. Things that mattered.

His business partner cracked jokes, filling the space while we orbited each other, pretending the ride down had not changed the shape of things.

But every time, he stood too close. Every time his hand brushed mine to pass a sample. There it was. That slow, unstoppable pull.

On the way back, the sky turned that washed-out Bali grey. Shrines blurred past us on the roadside. Offerings scattered by the wind. Burnt rubbish and ash.

"You are tired," he said as we stopped for petrol, his eyes sweeping over me in a way that felt too intimate for a petrol station.

"It has been a long day."

"You can rest," he offered. "I will get you home."

And I almost laughed.

How does someone surrender against the very thing unravelling them?

But I leaned in anyway.

Cheek against his back. Engine humming beneath us. Wind tugging at my hair. His heartbeat steady under my fingertips. Waves of something I did not have words for moved through me in time with the road.

And I melted into it.

If anyone had asked, I would have called it nothing.

But by the time we pulled into my driveway and I climbed off the bike, legs unsteady from something deeper than the ride, I realised…

This was not nothing.

This was already too much.

Chapter 8

WHEN THE STORM CAME

"And the day came when the risk to remain tight in a bud was more painful than the risk it took to blossom."
— **Anaïs Nin**

It started the way storms always do in Bali. Quiet at first. A wind slipping through the palm trees. A hush settling over the site. Workers muttering about getting home before the rain hit.

By midday, most of them were gone. Tools stowed. Tarps pulled tight over stacks of materials. Motorbikes buzzed one by one down the track until it was just us.

Just the two of us, standing in the hollowed-out shell of the villa.

No windows. No doors. Just open space and the low, steady rumble of thunder rolling off the mountains.

"You should go," I said, but my voice did not sound convincing, even to me.

He leaned against the frame of what would be the kitchen door. Arms crossed. Watching the sky darken.

"And leave you here alone?"

"I will not be far behind."

He looked at me, head tilted because he saw straight through the lie.

"Queen... come on."

I shook my head and turned back to whatever pointless task I had invented to keep my hands busy.

"Stop calling me that."

"But you are." His voice low, smooth as the air before the downpour. "You act like you are not, but you are."

And there it was again.

The shift.

The build.

The unspoken words.

Lightning split the sky. A flash of silver over the rice fields, where the paddies had turned bright green, heavy with the promise of what might come next.

Then the rain came.

Hard. Sudden. The path disappeared beneath it.

He moved. Not towards me. Not quite.

Just close enough that I felt it. The weight of him filling the space between us.

"You will get soaked," he said, and reached to tuck a strand of wet hair behind my ear.

He barely touched me.

And yet, it felt like the lightning had found my skin.

Everything in me paused.

"It is just rain," I whispered.

"You keep saying that."

And I did.

About the rain.

About him.

About us.

It is just the weather.

Just a joke.

Just harmless fun.

Except it was not.

And we both knew it.

A gust of wind tore through the villa, lifting dust and the sharp, metallic scent of wet cement.

We both turned and laughed.

For a second, it felt almost normal. Almost innocent. But then he looked at me. And I looked at him. And neither of us looked away.

"This is stupid," I said, quieter now.

"Yes."

"We should not."

"Probably not."

And yet neither of us moved.

"Looks like we are stuck," he said as if the gods themselves had not conspired to trap us here.

And somehow, no words were needed, we both understood.

This was the moment before the moment.

The last breath before the fall.

We could have walked away. Could have let it drift back into nothing.

But neither of us wanted to.

Not anymore.

Chapter 9

WAITING IT OUT

"Love, like rain, can nourish from above, drenching couples with a soaking joy. But sometimes, under the angry heat of life, love dries on the surface and must nourish from below, tending its roots."
— **Paulo Coelho**

Another storm. Another afternoon waiting it out.

The rain was relentless. A steady rhythm pounded the tiled roof, blurring the edges of the world.

The workers were long gone. The road already half-flooded.

"Looks like we're not going anywhere for a while," he said.

I nodded, wiping the rain from my forehead. Water slid down my back, soaking through cotton and linen until it clung to my body.

"Are you cold?"

"I'm fine."

We found shelter in the only finished room. Four walls. No windows. Just a roof.

He grabbed a wooden plank for a bench, and we sat side by side, facing the open doorway, and watched the rain fall like silver chains.

For a while, neither of us spoke.

Just the storm. The smell of wet earth. The occasional drip through the half-finished ceiling.

I fiddled with a loose thread on my dress, to avoid the piercing silence.

Out of the corner of my eye, I watched him. The way his forearm rested on his thigh. The way his head tilted down towards the floor. The quiet scrape of his thumb along the edge of his knee.

I should not have noticed that. I should not have been thinking about how easily that same thumb could trace the curve of my shoulder. My neck.

And yet.

And yet I sat there, absolutely still, absolutely burning. And he did not move closer. Did not utter a word.

We just waited.

Waited out the rain.

Waited out whatever else it was that kept us there.

Suspended.

Right on the edge of that thing neither of us dared touch.

"Is this what you imagined?" he asked eventually.

"The villa?"

He shrugged.

"All of it. Coming back to Bali. Building this life."

I thought about it. The years of planning. Sketches spread out on the kitchen table. The spreadsheets. The meetings. The persistent dream of my future nurtured. But I sat there, soaked and quivering, and realised in that moment, that exact, impossible moment, he had never been part of the design.

"Not exactly," I said.

He nodded like he already knew. Like maybe none of this was what he had planned either.

Outside, the rain shifted. The wind pushed it sideways, a fine mist reached us even in our hideout. I shivered before I could stop myself. He pulled off his jacket and draped it over my shoulders. His hands lingered just a beat too long on my arms.

"You don't have to."

"I know," he said. "Just... let me."

I let him.

I sat there in his jacket, breathed in the faint trace of clove and smoke. A part of me wondered if the rice beyond the villa would survive the heavy downpour. Whether the green could hold as it turned towards gold.

Neither of us moved.

Neither of us spoke.

It was not the right time. There was no need to say it out loud.

But if the rain had fallen all night, I'm not sure we could have stopped it.

Maybe that was the worst part. Knowing the longer we waited, the harder it would be to turn back.

And that moment was coming.

Soon.

Chapter 10

BEFORE THE DISTANCE

"Absence is to love what wind is to fire;
it extinguishes the small, it inflames the great."
— **Roger de Bussy-Rabutin**

Eventually, the rain slowed.

Not the kind of slow that feels like relief. The kind that feels like a warning. A pause before the sky remembers what it's supposed to be doing.

He checked his phone. The first time either of us acknowledged the world beyond these four damp walls.

"I should get going," he said.

And there it was. The weight of the unspoken. The thing neither of us dared name, but both felt pressing in from the corners.

His wife. The reason he could not stay.

I nodded as if it did not matter. As if I had not been silently hoping the storm might trap us there until morning. As if I had not already imagined what that night might have become.

"She will be wondering where you are?"

He shrugged. Putting on his helmet. Movements slow, reluctant, as if he was not quite ready to step back into whatever waited beyond the villa walls.

"It's not like that."

"It's exactly like that," I said, not unkindly, as I handed him back his jacket.

The paddies shimmered, stubborn in their cycle. Water, then green, then gold. And always, the inevitable cut.

Nothing stays suspended for long. Not even this.

For a moment, he just looked at me. A softness. A little tired. Like he wanted to say the thing, neither of us had the right to say.

And then he was gone.

The moan of his bike faded down the wet road, leaving me alone with the unfinished villa, the storm still hanging over everything, and the ache left behind.

And when I finally was ready to leave, I turned back. The house felt different.

Like the walls themselves had been holding their breath.

And now they knew.

Chapter 11

COMING TO MY SENSES

"The past is never where you think you left it."
— **Katherine Anne Porter**

I left Bali two weeks later.

Told myself it was just a trip home. To see family. To check in with the version of me that used to exist outside this island, this heat, this man.

In the UK, everything felt muted. Grey skies. Polite conversations. Supermarkets jarring under fluorescent lights, shelves full of stuff I did not want.

Nothing felt sharp.

Nothing felt real.

I thought distance would fix it. That an ocean and a continent might dissolve whatever had started growing between us.

But then he messaged me.

Hello my Queen. How are you? I have not heard from you for a long time, is everything alright?

Just a work update. The delivery had arrived. Did I like the bamboo blinds? What did I think of the video?

But the second I heard his voice, low and familiar, some quiet part of me snapped awake.

Like muscle memory.

Like heat under my skin.

Like my body had not forgotten.

The warmth of his hand on my arm.

The weight of his gaze lit from somewhere deeper than want.

I pressed the phone tighter to my ear as if I could close the miles. As if I could pull him through the speaker and into this cold, unfamiliar house.

My phone pinged again.

I miss you so much, my Queen.

Teasing, but I felt the tension beneath the words.

I smiled. Before I had time to think, I wrote back.

That's dangerous talk.

I know.

Ridiculous.

I felt like a teenager flirting through a screen, leaning into fantasies I had no business to feed.

But later, as I lay awake in my empty bed, I stopped pretending.

I missed him.

More than I wanted to admit.

I missed the way he looked at me like I was already his. And worse, I missed wanting to let him.

Outside the window, the rain fell in thin, grey sheets, nothing like the downpours back home. And I thought about the rice fields in Bali. How they would be ripening by now. Green giving way to gold. The slow, unstoppable pull toward harvest. Because that is the thing about longing. It grows whether you feed it or not.

And in some seasons, you cannot prevent the cut.

Chapter 12

BACK WHERE I STARTED

"You cannot swim for new horizons until you have courage to lose sight of the shore."
— William Faulkner

I told myself I had come back stronger. Clearer. Detached.

I practised it on the plane. Sat upright. Watched mediocre films. Drank tepid coffee. Pretended to sleep. Tried to believe I was back to who I was before it all started, as if 'before' still existed.

I repeated the story: It was nothing. Just boredom. Flattery. Heat. I imagined it.

But the moment I stepped onto the site and saw him — one hand in his pocket, shirt damp with humidity, that same grin curled at the edges of his mouth as he dragged on his cigarette — my whole performance collapsed.

"Queen," he said, like no time had passed at all. Like I had not crossed continents to try and forget him.

And that was it.

My body gave me away before I could stop it.

The polite version of me asked how things had been while I was gone. The rest of me just stood there, staring at the contours of his mouth. Wondering how it would feel to close the distance.

"I thought you might not come back," he said, quieter than usual.

"Neither did I."

We both laughed. Not because it was funny but because it was not.

I asked about the build. He pointed out the progress. Walls. Roof. The bones of the place filled in while I was gone.

I nodded along, but the question hovered between us the entire time.

What am I doing?

What are we doing?

And maybe worse. When do we finally stop pretending we are not already doing it?

When the others left, he lingered. Of course, he did.

"Stay a bit," he said.

I almost left.

Almost told him I was tired.

Almost remembered who I was supposed to be.

Instead, I stayed.

We sat on the steps of what would soon be the terrace, and watched the sky burn itself down over the rice fields. They shifted under the fading light, green touched with the first signs of gold.

"How was England?" he asked.

"Grey," I said. "Quiet. Cold."

"And now you're back in the chaos."

I nodded.

But what I did not say was: *I came back for you.* Because leaving had been impossible.

I wondered if his wife knew. If she felt the shift, the air thick with something, neither prayer nor duty could cleanse. And what right did I have to wonder? I was the guest. The invader. The woman with money, with options.

She stayed.

I would leave.

It was always going to end that way.

He reached down and picked up a stray petal from the offerings the workers had left behind. Turned it slowly between his fingers. And then, soft as a secret:

"I missed you."

I did not answer.

I did not have to.

The silence between had become a symphony.

Chapter 13

THE BOLDNESS

"Desire presses ever forward unsubdued."
— **Sigmund Freud**

It was no longer subtle.

A glance held a fraction too long. A hand steadying my back when it did not need to. A comment tossed loud enough for the others to hear but light enough that no one could be sure if it meant what it sounded like.

"Careful with that, Queen," he said one morning as I bent to inspect a kitchen cupboard. Voice low, smooth, pitched just enough to ripple through me.

"If you hurt yourself, I'll have to give you a proper massage."

His business partner snorted. The workers smirked behind their hands. I rolled my eyes, pretending I was not already flushed from head to toe.

But from that day on, he did not hold back. Not when others were around. Maybe, especially when others were around.

"I always miss you when you are not here," he called out one afternoon as I arrived. "Admit it, Queen. You hate it too when I am not here to look after you."

His partner laughed. So did I. My skin prickled, too obvious, too much.

"Oh god, here he goes again," I said, as breezy as I could manage, trying to eclipse my embarrassment.

Everyone laughed. Harmless. But under the surface, the silence vibrated with all the unspoken declarations.

And then the touches.

Quick. Casual. A brush of his fingers at my elbow. A palm at the small of my back as we pored over the plans. The back of his hand brushing mine as he passed me a pen, his thumb pressing just slightly into my wrist before letting go.

I told myself I was imagining it. But I was not.

The hum beneath my skin never shut off, a constant tremor tuned to a frequency I had not known existed.

Sunlight on the back of my neck felt indecent.

The breeze caressing my hair left me breathless.

The scent of sawdust, of damp earth, of his clove cigarettes curling into the afternoon air, intoxicating.

Everything sharp.

Everything alive.

Everything too much.

And the worst part?

I didn't want it to stop.

But I tried.

One evening, as the site emptied, we found ourselves alone just outside what would be my bedroom. The sky bruised purple at the edges, deep ultramarine that pooled in the corners of the sky, sienna bleeding into the horizon. Shadows stretched long across the floor. The light transformed everything in gold-leaf highlights and thick, inky black.

"You know they see it, right?" I declared, eyes fixed on the horizon.

"See what?" he said, stepping closer. Too close. His longing pushed into the space I had been pretending was mine.

"All of this." A nod toward that space between us. The glances. The pauses. The 'thing' neither of us had the nerve to name.

He tilted his head, smiling like he already knew exactly how far I would let him take it.

"Maybe I want them to."

And then he leaned in. Close enough that his breath caressed my face. Close enough that the whole world shrank to the inch between us.

I turned my face away.

"They will see," I whispered.

"So?"

I shook my head.

"Not yet."

He nodded once.

Slow.

Sure.

Eyes locked on mine like a promise.

"Soon."

And the worst part was, I knew he was right.

Soon…

And then I broke. Desire became louder than caution. Before I could talk myself out of it, I nodded toward the ensuite.

"I want to show you something before you go," I said, steady as anything.

Like it was just work.

Like this was nothing.

"Of course, boss," he said, playing along.

And I turned. Walked toward the bathroom.

I led.

He followed.

And the door closed behind us.

Chapter 14

THE KISS

"And then my soul saw you and it kind of went,
'Oh, there you are. I've been looking for you.'"
— **Unknown**

Inside the ensuite, the air felt thick.

Maybe it was the small space. Maybe the heat pressing through the open window. Or maybe it was just us.

Finally, out of sight.

Finally alone.

He turned slowly, leaned back against the counter, arms folded like he knew exactly why I had brought him here.

"What am I looking at?" he asked, voice low, amused.

I stepped closer. Close enough to see the gold flecks in his dark eyes. Close enough to smell salt on his skin, the faint trace of clove and smoke that clung to his clothes.

But the game had run its course. I let the silence stretch long enough to feel dangerous.

"You have been talking a lot," I said softly.

He smiled. "Have I?"

I nodded. "So much teasing. So many declarations."

Another step closer. Slow. Deliberate. His breath carried the sweet burn of Sampoerna cigarettes.

Before either of us could make another joke, I slid my hands to his face.

He stilled.

Eyes wide.

Waiting.

And then I kissed him.

Just like that.

Not rushed. Not wild. A slow, sure press of my mouth to his. A quiet claiming. *See? This is how it is done.*

And that was all it took.

He was gone. His hands in my hair. On my back. Pulling me into him like we were long overdue.

My fingers twisted in his shirt. Dragging him closer until there was nothing left between us.

Heat.

Teeth.

Breath.

The scrape of stubble rasped low against my throat. The weight of him, solid and certain, as if our bodies had waited for this precise moment to remember how they fit.

We did not speak.

We did not need to.

And then, just as suddenly, I pulled back.

One last taste.

One final look.

Then I let him go.

"Right," I said, adjusting my dress, running a hand through my hair like that might undo any of it.

"You should probably get going." I tilted my chin toward his partner, who was finishing up for the day.

He blinked, dazed. "You are sending me home?"

I smiled. Slow. Wicked.

"We don't want people talking."

He laughed, shaking his head like I had knocked the air from his lungs.

And then he left.

I stood alone in the bathroom, fingertips resting against my lips, heart pounding like I had stolen something I was never meant to touch.

And maybe I had.

Chapter 15

THE HUM

"The body remembers what the mind forgets."
— **Martha Manning**

After the kiss, everything altered.

Not just inside me. The whole world became surreal. As if someone had peeled back the skin of reality and turned the volume to full.

The undercurrent inside me would not stay calm.

It roared.

Constant.

Everywhere.

Walking through the market the next morning felt illicit. I was not thinking about him, not exactly. I was feeling the bliss of his mouth under mine.

About how I had started it.

And how he had followed.

About how my body had not come down since.

The air clung like hands. The fruit sellers' voices slid down my spine like silk. A papaya split open on a stall, sweet and lush and dripping, sent a low and liquid shiver through me.

Everything shimmered.

Tamarind sharp on my tongue, coriander and chillies lingered at the back of my throat. Woodsmoke drifted from the Warungs, curling, slow and easy.

Heat pooling between my shoulder blades.

The breeze caressing my body.

Motorbikes growled past, low and steady, like they knew.

It was not just him anymore. It was the whole world.

The sun-kissed back of my neck.

The earth itself pulsed beneath my feet.

Even the rice fields seemed to breathe.

Green unfolding towards gold, that slow, inevitable ripening, as if the land was feeling it too.

And people noticed. Or maybe I was finally paying attention.

Lingering looks. Passing smiles. The brush of a stranger's hand at the till, not pulling away too fast.

And it did not feel dangerous. It did not feel like something to apologise for. It felt like power. As if wanting had made me magnetic. As if desire itself had turned me into light.

I rode through the streets, skin warm, air rushing past, every part of me wide open. Alive in a way I had almost forgotten.

Grateful.

Weightless.

As if I had woken up to myself without even realising I had gone.

On-site, he barely pretended. The moment I arrived, his eyes met mine. Greedy. Unashamed. Like we were still locked inside that bathroom, my hands on his skin, his mouth burning against mine.

"You are glowing today," he said.

Too loud.

Too casual.

While the others hammered tiles onto the roof.

I grinned. Because it was not a compliment. It was the truth. I could feel it. Buzzing through me. Filling the empty spaces. This was not about being pretty. Or sexy. Or any of those thin, breakable words. This was the world rearranging itself around the pulse of me.

At night, I could not switch it off. The air thick and still. Sheets rough against skin that felt too awake to rest. Eyes closed, but his hands were still there. The echo of his mouth. The weight of his longing. And I did not know where the hunger started anymore. Where it ended. Or if it ever would. And part of me did not want it to. Part of me wanted to live inside this forever.

Half-wild.

Half-drunk.

Completely awake.

Chapter 16

OUR SECRET

"We all have secrets we'll never tell."
— **Unknown**

The days that followed looked the same. And yet, everything had changed.

The site buzzed as always. Wheelbarrows scraped over gravel. Voices raised over the clang of metal and some distant ballad drifted from an old radio.

His business partner waved when I arrived. Someone handed me coffee. The sun beat down. The work moved forward. As if the kiss had never happened.

But the moment I saw him, self-control vanished.

He did not say a word. Just that look. That grin. Like we were the only two people in on the joke.

And I suppose we were.

The banter softened.

What had been play was replaced by something else. Something real.

"Morning, Queen," he said, his eyes carrying the memory of my hands on his face, his mouth on mine.

"Morning," I answered, the smile already there before I could prevent it.

The rest of the day, we circled each other.

Standing too close.

Comparing measurements that did not need comparing. Passing tools, our fingers brushing, pausing, holding.

And when no one was looking, he leaned in. Close enough for his breath to skim my neck.

"This is ours now," he whispered like it was obvious.

I looked up at him. And that was enough.

Something passed between us, silent and certain, as if we had both asked the same question at the same time.

"All of it?"

He nodded.

And that was all I needed.

Maybe I should have felt nervous.

Or guilty.

Or afraid.

But I did not.

I felt alive.

Like the world had quietly rearranged itself to make space for us.

A secret place, just big enough to hold what was unfolding.

Later, when I caught him watching me from across the site, I tilted my head, raised an eyebrow.

"*What?*" I mouthed.

And he smiled, slow and sure.

"*Everything*," he mouthed back.

And that was the moment I realised I did not need more than this.

Not promises.

Not futures.

Not answers to questions better left unasked.
Just him.
Exactly as he was.
Exactly as we were.
Our secret.
And somehow, that felt like enough.

Chapter 17

TOO MUCH

"I want to do with you what spring does
with the cherry trees."
— **Pablo Neruda**

It did not take long before we stopped the performance.

At least not with each other.

With the rest of the world? Of course.

We were polite.

Careful.

A little space between our bodies when his partner walked past. A neutral tone when we spoke about where to position the plug sockets and light switches.

But underneath it? Behind the easy smiles and the casual nods? We were already gone.

I stayed late that day. Made some excuse about finalising the lighting plan. As if it could not wait until morning.

We did not notice the last streaks of daylight bleed out, and the sky darkened fast, the way it always does here.

One moment, gold slipped over the rice. The next, night fell hard.

The workers had gone.

His partner, too.

But he stayed.

"We should go," I said, even though I did not mean it.

Even though my whole body ached from the effort of not closing the last inch between us.

Even though I had spent the entire day balanced on the edge of falling, trying to remember I was supposed to be the one in charge.

He looked up from where he crouched by the terrace steps, wiping dust from his palms, sweat shining along his hairline.

"No," he said.

Simple.

Certain.

And that was it.

We sat together on the veranda, a light breeze caught the banana leaves, making them rustle like rain. I sipped from the water bottle he handed me, grateful to have something for my hands to do. The night filled itself in around us. Frogs waking in the paddies. Crickets stitching the dark together. The soft rattle of palm fronds overhead.

And him.

Always him.

My body surged low and steady. Weeks of restraint clenched in my stomach. I crossed my legs, as if that might contain the ache that was impossible to ignore.

I had not painted in months. Had not picked up a pencil or a brush. There was no space left for it. Desire had eaten all the edges. Left me too full of him to hold anything else.

At some point, his hand found my knee. Just rested there. Like it belonged.

And I let it.

We did not speak for a long time. There was no need. The weight of him erased the gap I had been clinging to.

Finally, he turned towards me.

"You feel it, too?"

I nodded. Because, of course, I did. It was all I felt anymore.

"It's too much," I whispered.

He smiled, slow and wicked.

"Yeah," he said. "It is."

But neither of us moved.

Neither of us pulled back.

And when his thumb slid over the inside of my knee, slow circles on bare skin, I thought,

Let it be too much.

Let it take everything.

Because by then, I did not want balance.

Did not want sense.

Did not want rules or reasons or the quiet safety of waiting.

I just wanted him.

Right there.

Right then.

Forever, if the night allowed.

Chapter 18

BREAKING POINT

"To burn with desire and keep quiet about it is the greatest punishment we can bring on ourselves."
— **Federico García Lorca**

The villa was nearly finished. Clean lines. Fresh paint. Polished floors. It should have felt like an ending, but all I felt was the weight of his attention from across the room.

Steady.

Dark.

Barely contained.

He was meant to be walking me through the final details. Instead, he watched me like we had already agreed on something neither of us had said aloud.

"Looks good," I said, pretending to care about the new rattan lampshades.

"Yeah," he replied, but his eyes never left me.

His partner waited by the front gate, scrolling through his phone. Blissfully unaware.

And yet, here we were. Alone in the living room. Late afternoon, gold spilling through the glass doors. The air still and heavy, like it knew what was coming.

I turned to say something.

Something ordinary.

Something about deliveries or deadlines, but the words barely made it out.

He was already there.

Closing the space between us.

Sliding an arm around my waist.

Pulling me in like it was the most natural thing in the world.

And then his mouth was on mine.

Soft at first. Testing. But it did not stay soft for long.

The hunger crept up fast. Pushed out of him. Poured into me.

I felt it everywhere.

The shift of his breath.

The slide of his hands down my back.

The press of his body.

Solid.

Certain.

Impossible to ignore.

A laugh almost escaped me, but it died against his lips.

The kiss deepened.

Open.

Sure.

Like he had waited years and did not intend to waste another second.

I was still his boss. Still the woman who had signed his contract. Still the one responsible for this whole damn project.

But none of it mattered. Not with his hands on my body. His mouth tracing down my neck. His thigh pressing between mine, shifting me back against the wall like we both knew we could not stop.

Maybe the stopping part was already behind us.

When I finally managed to breathe, I whispered the only warning left.

"Someone might come in."
He smiled against my skin.
"So let them."
And just like that, I knew.
We were not turning this around.
Not now.
Not ever.

Chapter 19

THE WAITING FIELDS

"Nothing human loves forever."
— Zadie Smith

Morning arrived too bright. Too honest.

I arrived on site early and stood watching the paddies beyond glisten in their final stretch of gold, heavy with the promise of harvest. The weight of the grain bending the stalks toward the earth. The cut was close. The air smelled of wet earth and endings.

Soon, the blades would come. The fields would be stripped bare. The mud left raw and exposed beneath the sun.

We moved around each other carefully that day.

Not avoiding.

Not apologising.

Just... slower. As if the night before might still be clinging to our skin, and neither of us wanted to rub it off too fast.

Outside, I watched the farmers walk the edges of the fields, heads low, calculating the days left before they reaped what had bloomed.

And I wondered how long we had. How many nights? How many more stolen hours before the blades came out?

The cycle turns.

That is what it does.
Green to gold.
Gold to gone.
And after?
Nothing but the stubble and dust.

Chapter 20

THE FALL

"Some things cannot be unsaid, undone, or unfelt."
— UNKNOWN

It was inevitable.

We never schedule our undoing. It simply finds us.

The villa was empty. The workers had long gone. The sky outside held the last sliver of daylight, gold drained into indigo. The fields beyond lay still, the rice heavy, on the cusp of harvest.

Inside, the space was unfinished. No furniture. No doors. Just walls waiting to be filled. Shadows lurked in the corners like accomplices.

Like us.

Waiting.

I should have left. I even said it out loud.

"I must go."

And he just looked at me. As if the idea was absurd. As if there was no version of this night where I walked away.

"You are not going anywhere," he said.

So I stayed.

One moment, we were standing by the doorway. The next, his hands were on my hips. My back met the cool plaster. His body pinned me there as if gravity had stopped pretending it was not involved.

This time, there was no pause. No testing the edges. The kiss landed hard, open, unrepentant.

Teeth.

Tongue.

Low sounds pressed into the skin just below my ear, making me shiver.

He tasted of sweat and cigarettes and the kind of craving that turns a person wild. Like something I had been desiring for so long, I could no longer remember what it felt like to want anything else.

When his hands slid beneath my skirt, rough palms dragging up my thighs, I did not stop him. The wanting had been living between us for months. Stalking us through every glance, every offhand joke, every fleeting touch. And now it had nowhere left to go but out.

Loud.

Unruly.

Inevitable.

His mouth found the curve of my neck. The hollow of my collarbone. Hands sliding, palms mapping my body as if learning the shape of something sacred.

When I reached for his shirt, he caught my wrists. Held them still for a moment, just long enough for me to feel his pulse, the quiet tremor of restraint unravelling.

Then he let me.

Clothes peeled away. Skin met skin. Heat met heat. He was already hard. He pressed against me, no longer subtle, no longer pretending this was something he could control.

No hesitation.

Just hunger.

Deep.

Slow.

The kind of hunger that had nothing to do with taking and everything to do with knowing.

I felt him everywhere.

He groaned into my mouth as I shifted, rolling my hips up to meet him. Once. Just enough to break us both open.

"Fuck," he whispered. "You are going to kill me."

But I did not feel merciful.

Not anymore.

His fingers slipped under the edge of my knickers as if they had always belonged there. And I was ready for him.

Wet.

Open.

No hesitation.

No question.

Like my body had been waiting for this moment to be allowed.

I let go.

Let him unmake me.

He worked me open, slow at first. Testing the shape of me. Feeling how ready I already was. And when I could no longer take the waiting, I tilted my hips into him, wordless, needing him closer, needing all of him.

I fumbled for his belt. For the button. For anything that would close the distance faster. And then there was nothing left between us.

We moved like we had minutes to live.

Fast.

Clumsy.

Desperate.

My back arched off the wall as he held me there, lifted me as if I was weightless. And when he finally moved inside me, when we gave in completely, it was not wild or frantic.

It was something else entirely.

All the weeks.

All the waiting.

All the wanting.

Filling me until the boundaries blurred between his body ending and mine beginning. Until breathing was optional.

Like we had stepped into something timeless.

A rhythm older than us. Older than anything.

And still, some distant part of me heard the outside world. A bike coughing to life on the road. A voice calling out from somewhere I did not care to place.

But none of it mattered.

Because this was ours.

The secret we had made.

The place we had built.

And I wanted him.

All of him.

Here.

Now.

For as long as the night would allow.

And in that moment, as the night folded around us, I realised:

This was not just desire.

This was devotion.

And still, it was not enough.

I wanted more.

Harder.

Deeper.

As if I could make him disappear inside me. As if I could swallow the whole of him and make the craving stop.

He moved like a man starved. No patience left. No fear of being caught. My skirt bunched at my waist, forgotten. His jeans halfway down his thighs.

Nothing elegant.

Nothing careful.

Just bodies.

Colliding.

Gripping.

Grinding.

The edge of the wall digging into my back. My legs wrapped around his hips, holding him there, dragging him closer, closer. I bit down on his shoulder to keep from crying out. Felt his fingers tighten on my thighs in answer. Felt him pulse inside me, harder now, rougher, like neither of us could keep pace with the need anymore.

It built fast. Too fast. Like a storm breaking open inside my very being.

I did not want it to end.

But I could not hold it back. Not when his mouth found my neck again, teeth scraping the skin like a warning. Not when I heard him curse under his breath, the sound low and broken and meant only for me.

I dug my nails into his back. Tilted my hips higher. Took everything he gave me and asked for more.

And when it finally hit, it ripped through me like lightning.

Sharp.

Bright.

Total.

For a moment, I forgot where we were. Who we were. Why this was supposed to matter.

This ruinous, perfect fusion.

And even as we slowed, as the air thickened around us, as the sound of night crawled back through the cracks, neither of us moved.

We stayed locked there. Breathless. Pinned.

His cock still inside me, both of us trembling with the force of it.

Neither of us spoke. What was there to say?

The room was dense with sweat and dust and something almost animal. The taste of him still on my tongue. The smell of skin and smoke and sex clinging to the walls.

I felt his heartbeat against my chest, wild and uneven. Felt his breath hot on my neck. Felt the last shudders run through both of us, like aftershocks.

No one had come looking. The night held us there, quiet and complicit.

For a moment, I wanted to stay like that forever. Pinned to the wall. Wrapped around him. Lost inside the thing we had finally stopped fighting.

But slowly, the world began to return.

A motorbike passed on the road. A gecko clicking from the rafters. The distant bark of a stray dog reminding us where we were.

He eased back just enough to look at me. Hair damp. Lips swollen. That crooked, impossible grin like he could not believe we had actually done it.

I lowered my skirt with shaking hands. Wiped the sweat from my forehead, as if that might undo the obvious. Like any of this could be hidden.

I could have felt embarrassed. I could have felt regret.

But I did not.

I felt wrecked. Ravenous. Stripped bare and starving for more.

"Are you okay, my Queen?" he asked, voice low and rough.

I nodded. Because I was. Better than okay.

"Yeah," I whispered.

"Yeah."

And for once, neither of us pretended it was nothing.

Because now, it was not.

Now, it was everything.

Chapter 21

THE AFTERMATH

"The land remembers who it belongs to,
even when men forget."
— **Balinese Saying**

The next morning, I woke sore. Not from the work. Not from the heat. From him.

From all the ways my body had been pushed open, filled, emptied, and filled again.

The ache was not pain. It was proof.

Proof that we had finally crossed the line we had been toeing for months. Proof that I had not imagined any of it.

Everything felt different in the daylight. Brighter. Exposed.

The villa was finished, except for the final touches. The furniture was scheduled to arrive, and I would move in.

I walked the rooms alone. Bare feet on cool tiles. Fingers trailing over freshly painted walls. Trying to make sense of the dream almost built, and the thing we had just unravelled.

But all I could feel was him.

Clouds still hung low from the night before, thick and humid. The rice was ready. The harvest had begun. You could feel the strain in the stalks, the way they tipped just a little too far, exhausted by their own abundance.

And me? I felt the same. Unleashed. Hollowed out. A body still echoing with what had happened inside these walls.

The men moved through the brittle stalks, blades slicing through gold. Bundling what was left into piles. I watched them work.

Rows fell cleanly. One after another. Orderly. Predictable. Leaving the earth exposed and raw, drying under the weight of what had been taken.

The cycle doing what it always does.

Maybe I should have felt regret.

Instead, I only felt the ghost of him still inside me. And the impossible fact that I somehow knew this was not the peak. It was only the beginning.

His voice was careful that morning. Measured. While mine stumbled over apologies, I did not speak. Because the truth sat between us, obvious as the rising sun.

I could choose how this ended.

He could not.

He took me in, slow, deliberate. Enough to say yes, it happened. Yes, it is still happening.

And as the workers dragged their blades through the paddies, I stood at the edge of the terrace and watched the gold fall.

They worked the fields while I looked on. Their hands knew this land in ways mine never would. And yet here I was, the one who owned it. On paper, at least. Maybe that was the oldest story of all. Take what was never yours. Call it progress. Call it love.

But the fields between us knew better.

The cycle had shifted. The damage done.

And somewhere in the mud beneath our feet, the next season was already waiting.

We waited, too. In the silence after wanting.

In the ache that comes when nothing is left to take but each other.

Maybe I would let the fields rest a while. Leave the earth to crack and breathe. See what might grow on its own. What else was there to do?

Cut.

Clear.

Leave the earth bare until the water comes back.

Chapter 22

THE SLOW BURN

"Whatever our souls are made of,
his and mine are the same."
— **Emily Bronte, *Wuthering Heights***

The next time was not rushed.

No one waited at the gate.

No footsteps on the path.

No excuses left to leave.

Just us.

And this time, we did not tear at each other. We unfolded.

He touched me like he had been waiting his whole life to remember how. Fingers gliding down the length of my arm, pausing at my wrist as if listening for something. Palms settling on my hips like they belonged there.

No urgency.

No end goal.

Just the quiet pulse of skin meeting skin.

We lay side by side on fresh white linen. The villa finished around us at last. The night slipping through open windows, warm and fragrant with frangipani and bonfires.

Still, the current of him rose in me. Quiet. Unstoppable. Like something waking up, stretching its limbs after a lifetime asleep.

When his hand moved down to my ankle, barely touching, a tremor shot straight through me. A slow, shimmering heat that spiralled upward, gathering at the base of my spine, winding higher.

The lightest touch, his thumb drifting from my shoulder to my forearm, and the whole of me lit up. Quiet and sudden, like striking a match in the dark.

Not like arousal. It was much deeper. Older. Like a current that run the length of me, humming through every nerve.

I realised then what it was. All these months of ripples and restlessness. The quiver in my belly. The tension I could not name. Now uncoiling. Rising. Flooding me with a sensation so acute, so slow, I could barely hold it.

Was it Kundalini?

The Goddess?

Or something else entirely.

It felt cosmic.

He did not rush. Did not push. Just kept finding new ways to drag his hands over me like I was some secret he was still learning to read.

His lips followed, mapping every place the light flooded. The line of my collarbone. The hollow of my throat. The soft inside of my forearm. The dip below my ribs that made my whole body flutter.

And lower still. To the curve of my hips. To the place between my thighs where the inferno waited, patient, craving.

He opened me slowly, carefully, as if I were a precious jewel. His mouth followed, deliberate and unhurried, tasting me like he meant to stay there forever. Like I might vanish if he moved too fast.

He tasted me like worship. Like hunger slowed to reverence. Like he was not there to take but to stay.

As if every part of me deserved time. As if there was nowhere else to be but here.

And I let him. Opened for him. Offered him everything.

Let him draw the heat higher, deeper, until the edges of me blurred, and there was only breath, and the silent ache that had nowhere else to go.

In that moment, I felt more than wanted.

I felt seen.

As if every scar and story my body carried was worth knowing.

I let him explore me like sacred ground. Every part of me offered. Nothing hidden. Nothing hurried.

And still, he did not stop. Not when I arched beneath him. Not when I whispered his name into the dark. Not until my body came apart in waves so ethereal and slow, it felt like being carried out to sea.

And even then, he stayed.

Hands on my thighs. Breath against my skin. Holding me there, open and surrendered, as if I was the only thing left worth tending to.

And when his hands had mapped enough of my body, when his mouth had tasted enough of my ecstasy, I turned him onto his back. Shifted my weight over him, straddling his hips.

And when I had taken everything he gave me, I wanted to give it back. All of it. Every tremor he had built inside me. Every pulse he had woken up. To taste him. To know him that way.

I kissed the curve of his shoulder. The hollow of his throat. The line of his jaw where the stubble rasped softly under my lips. His eyes closed, his body loose beneath me, trusting. Like I could do anything, and he would let me.

And I did.

I took my time. Rolled my hips against him, lazy and unhurried, not to rush it, but to feel the full weight of him beneath me.

I trailed my fingers down his stomach, over the sharp dip of his hips, down to where he was already waiting for me. Hard and certain and impossibly warm.

I stroked him slowly, reverently. Like art. Like prayer. Like something sacred that I had been entrusted to care for.

And he let me.

Breathing harder now, his hands rested on my thighs, not to guide me, only to stay connected.

I moved over him slowly. Kissed down the length of his stomach, feeling the tension coil beneath his skin.

When I wrapped my mouth around him, I did it without haste, without noise, with nothing but reverence. Like devotion. Like thanks. Like memorising him from the inside out.

I worked him with my lips, my tongue, my hands. Not to finish him, but to hold him there, right on the edge of losing himself, of giving in.

And the sounds he made, low, broken, barely there, were their own kind of reward.

I wanted him laid bare. I wanted to worship the length of him, slow and deliberate until he forgot his own name.

And when he pulled me back up, breathless and shaking, it was not to stop me. It was to have me again. All of me. Every part.

When I finally took him inside me, it felt like coming home. Our bodies slotting together, built for this exact union. This exact night.

We moved together like water.

Leisurely.

Endless.

Rising and falling.

Breath syncing.

Hearts matching pace until there was no space left between us.

We stayed like that.

Moving in slow, unhurried waves.

No chasing the end.

Just staying inside the swell, the ripple, the long, golden stretch of pleasure for pleasure's sake.

It was not just lust. Not just desire. But something quieter. Something holy. A kind of worship neither of us had words for.

And the orgasms came in waves. Soft at first. Then rolling. Tearing through me one after another, as if my body had become its own language of pleasure. As if the whole night had been building to this release I could not contain, did not want to.

It did not stop. Not really. Every touch became a new beginning. Every kiss, another circuit closed.

Hours passed.

Or maybe lifetimes.

We stayed tangled together, chasing the next high or maybe just resting inside the one we had not yet come down from.

Breathing the same ecstasy.

When it slowed, and finally we let stillness find us again, I pressed my face into his shoulder. He kissed the top of my head like we had always been this way. Like this was what we were meant for.

No guilt.

No questions.

No names for what we had made.

Just us.

Two bodies.

One secret.

Breathing.

Waiting for the next time.

Because we both knew there would be one.

And another.

And another.

Chapter 23

THE TIPPING POINT

"We are all just walking each other home."
— **Ram Dass**

We stayed there long after it ended.

If you could even call it an ending.

The night had folded itself around us, suspended in silence, the village sounds caught in the hush of it. The air smelled of burnt incense and rain, although we never really heard it fall. His hand drifted over my back in slow, absent circles, like he was not ready to stop touching me, even in sleep.

Neither of us moved. Neither of us spoke. It felt as if words might shatter whatever spell we had fallen into.

We had not just fucked.

We had fallen.

Somewhere deeper than either of us intended.

I watched the ceiling fan turn shadows across the plaster, thin and weightless as ghosts.

Thought about leaving. Gathering my clothes. Slipping out before we had time to name the thing hovering between us.

But I stayed.

I was home.

Instead, I turned my head and looked at him.

And he was already looking at me.

"What are we doing?" I asked.

It was not an accusation. Not even a question. Just a quiet wondering.

Because none of this made sense. It could not.

And yet, here we were. Breathless. Naked. Changed.

He smiled. Faint. Tired.

"I do not know," he said. "But I do not want it to end."

Neither did I.

God, neither did I.

And maybe that was enough.

Maybe we did not need to call it anything.

Maybe it only had to exist like this.

A hidden world.

Outside reason.

Beyond rules.

By now, even the gods looked away.

The offerings wilted on their plates.

The incense burned down to the stick.

I rested my head on his chest, listening to the slow, steady rhythm beneath his skin.

And for the first time in years, I felt safe. Not chasing. Not searching. Just still.

Maybe it would not last. Maybe it never could.

But right then, I did not care.

Right then, it was all I wanted.

Chapter 24

THE MORNING AFTER

"There is always some madness in love. But there is also always some reason in madness."
— Friedrich Nietzsches

He did not rush to leave.

For once, there was no pretending we had somewhere else to be.

The light came in slowly, slipping through the open windows, unfiltered and silver, touching the bare walls like a blessing.

I stretched beneath the thin sheet, the air still cool from the night, and watched him move around the room.

Barefoot. Shirtless. At home here, in a way I had not quite managed, even though I owned it.

He was not trying to impress me. He was not trying at all. And maybe that was why it felt so devastating. Because it was not performative. It was just him. Filling the space with his quiet presence. Carrying two mugs of strong, black coffee as if it was the most natural thing in the world.

"For you, my Queen," he said, placing one on the bedside table beside me.

And I laughed, shaking my head, but the name no longer annoyed me the way it once had. It felt tender now. As if maybe he meant it.

We sat side by side on the mattress, backs against the bedhead, watching the rice fields awaken through the open glass doors.

And for a little while, we needed no words.

We just sipped coffee and let the morning hold us.

I noticed things I had not before.

The faint scar along his shoulder.

The way his knee twitched slightly when he was thinking.

The softness in the way he beheld me when the show was over, when it was only us.

"What?" he asked when he caught me looking.

"Nothing," I said.

But it was not nothing. It was never nothing.

It was the terrifying, aching sense that I did not want this to end.

That this quiet, stolen morning, this warmth, this easiness was starting to feel dangerously close to resembling home. And that thought should have scared me. Should have made me pull away. Remind myself of all the reasons this was impossible.

But I remained.

I just leaned my head on his shoulder. And he kissed the top of it like he had done it a thousand times before. And for now, that was enough.

For now, we were still inside the dream.

The secret was still ours.

And the world had not come knocking yet.

Chapter 25

CRACKS IN THE DREAM

"Some things are too wild to name.
Too beautiful to tie down."
— **Atticus**

We had shared so many long, delicious moments by now. A few stolen nights. A handful of mornings where he managed to stay, slipping home later than he should, leaving me wrapped in sheets that still smelled of him.

For a while, it felt endless. As if we could stretch this secret until the season broke. Until the fields flooded again, and the whole thing washed clean.

But the harvest had already come.

The paddies lay cracked and dry now. All that soft green promise gone. The water drained. The mud baked hard beneath the sun.

And us?

We were still here. But not the same.

Something had been taken. Cut clean.

The nights had softened. The touches lingered but with an echo of goodbye behind them.

He still came. I still stayed.

But I felt the air between us thinning.

And still, he stayed the whole night again.

No whispered plans to slip out early. No nervous flickers towards the door. Just sleep. And waking. And coffee. And me pretending not to wonder how he would explain the missing hours. Because he had to, didn't he? Somewhere, someone was waiting.

As much as I wanted to believe we were still floating inside our secret, I felt the weight of it pressing down.

The unspoken questions. The ticking clock.

When he finally stood to leave, pulling his shirt over his head, the moment lingered longer than it should.

"I will see you tomorrow?" I asked, as if we still had forever. But the project was finished, apart from any final fixes I discovered. The workers had packed up. The villa complete.

And after that?

The wife. The life waiting for him on the other side of all this. The place where I did not belong.

He smiled and kissed my forehead tenderly.

"I will come during the day. After the handover. When no one is here."

And I nodded. But something in me shifted. A small, sharp pang. The quiet recognition of an ending already unfolding. The fantasy was beginning to fray. Just at the edges. Barely. But I felt it. And I knew the only way to keep it alive was to hold tighter. To keep pretending. To keep wanting. To keep taking every stolen moment until there were no moments left to steal.

So I kissed him once more before he left.

Slow.

Deep.

Final, in a way, neither of us wanted to acknowledge.

"Come back tomorrow," I whispered.

And he nodded like there was no question.

But when the door shut behind him, the morning light felt harsher.

And I wondered how long the dream could hold.

Chapter 26

THE DAY VISIT

"I have loved in life and I have been loved.
I have drunk the cup of life to the very dregs.
Yet always I thirst."
— **Oscar Wilde**

The builders were long gone.

Off to another site, another project, their laughter and shouts drifting into someone else's morning now.

And just like that, the villa was mine.

The quiet settled in first. Then, the space. Then, the stillness that comes when there is finally nothing left to do but breathe and look out at the impossible view.

Rice fields stretching forever. The sky unrolling itself in endless shades of gold and pink. The light so beautiful it hurt.

And for a little while, it felt perfect.

A bubble of beauty. Of passion. Of longing. That prolonged ecstasy of being suspended in a secret, heightened world, where everything feels surreal, intoxicating, too good.

Where time bends.

Where consequences disappear.

Except they do not.

And I felt them creeping in that day. Sneaky and steady, just below the surface.

He arrived in the early afternoon, helmet dangling by the strap, sweat at his temples, and that same intoxicating grin.

But the energy was different this time.

It was not playful.

It was not bold.

It was... careful.

Because there were no more workers to hide behind. No noise to cover the sounds we made. No reason for him to be here except the one neither of us said out loud.

"You are alone?" he asked as if he did not quite believe it.

"All mine," I said, gesturing to my dream. "At least until they come back for any final fixes."

I was already trying to find excuses for him to return.

He nodded, stepped inside, and the door closed behind him with a click that felt louder than it should.

For a while, we acted normal. Or tried to.

We walked through the rooms. Checked the finishes. Pretended this was still just a project.

But the silence pressed in too boldly. And when we stood in the living room, looking out at the fields, he reached for me without hesitation. Like we were picking up a conversation we had never actually started.

His hands slid around my back. I leaned into him, my body already humming. But this time, I felt the weight of it. The strangeness. The risk.

His wife was not far from my thoughts. Nor was the question I had not yet asked.

What happens now the villa is finished?

When the work dries up?

When the excuses run out?

And yet, I did not stop him. Did not pull away. Because the dream was still clinging. Just barely.

And I was not ready to wake up. Not yet.

So I turned in his arms and kissed him like the world outside did not exist.

Like this could last.

And maybe, just for that afternoon, it did.

Chapter 27

THE LAST DAY OF THE SECRET

"And even as I watch it slip through my fingers, I do not wish it unmade."
— **Atticus**

We never spoke of endings. Never dared.

Instead, we lived as if we could stretch the golden hours forever. If we stayed soft enough, slow enough, the world might move on without us.

The villa had been our cocoon. Empty now except for me and him when he came.

No workers.

No deadlines.

No repairs.

Just footsteps echoing across smooth floors, the moan of wind through open windows.

He arrived in the afternoons when the heat softened and the light began its descent. Always unannounced. Always certain I would be there.

And I was.

We stopped pretending it was about the project. There was nothing left to check, nothing left to fix. Just us, moving through the empty rooms we had made together.

He touched the walls like they meant something. Brushed dust from the countertops. Ran his fingers along the terrace rail, watching the fields sway in the breeze.

"This place feels like ours," he said once.

And for a moment, I let myself believe him.

That this secret, this slow, aching paradise we had built, belonged to us.

But even the evenings felt shorter now.

He lingered for a while, long enough to boil noodles and press his lips to the back of my neck as the sun slid into the fields, but not much more.

We moved slowly. Spoke less. Touched more.

No urgency.

No ripping buttons open.

No frantic hands.

Just long, wandering mouths, trying to memorise the feeling before the season turned.

But somewhere beneath the sweetness, I felt it coming.

The end.

Waiting like a shadow behind the door.

Not today.

Not yet.

But soon.

And so I kissed him like I could hold it off. Like if I kissed him deeply enough, we might stay here.

Weightless.

Endless.

Outside of time.

Chapter 28

THE SILENCE IN BETWEEN

"And ever has it been known that love knows not its own depth until the hour of separation."
— **Kahlil Gibran**

Days passed.

Long, golden, silent days.

The villa held its breath. As if it knew we were nearing the inevitable. Or maybe just the end of this chapter, the secret, suspended part where everything felt endless in the eternal present. The work was done. The rooms finished. The days quieter than they should have been. And he did not come as often anymore.

There were reasons, of course. Other projects. Other obligations. Other rooms he belonged in that were not mine.

But the space he left behind felt too wide. Too loud.

I found myself standing on the veranda more often, watching the road across the paddies for the sound of his bike. Checking my phone, even when I knew he would not call. Inventing excuses to message, to remind him I was still here, waiting in the place we built together.

And when he did come, it was like slipping back into water after holding your breath too long.

Relief.

Saturation.

That feeling returning.

But when he left again, the quiet was worse. The silence pressed deeper into the walls. Into me.

And the sunsets, God, the sunsets were excruciating now. They stretched out in those impossible colours, bleeding into the fields as if they mocked me. All this beauty, and no one to share it with except the ghost of him.

I sat alone on the terrace as dusk slid its soft hands over the fields. Legs curled beneath me. The last light fading. The air soft. The night emerging slowly. And I thought about how quickly it had all happened. How easily I had fallen into this. How much I had let myself want. And what exactly I was waiting for now. Because I did not want promises. I did not want marriage. I did not even want more than what we had.

But I wanted him.

Here.

Now.

Again.

And the wanting was starting to ache. The secret was still ours. But secrets are heavy things when you have to hold them alone.

And later, as the paddies lay stripped and flattened, the ground dried to cracked mud, the frogs grew quiet, and the offerings turned to brittle petals in the heat, I wondered if we had missed the signs. If we were already past the part where it all keeps growing.

Because soon, there would be nothing left but the waiting.

The aching pause.

The knowing look across an empty field, where something used to be but was not anymore.

And the gods would turn their backs once again.

Chapter 29

WHEN HE COMES BACK

"We loved with a love that was more than love."
— **Edgar Allan Poe**

It had been long enough that I had almost convinced myself I was okay. That I did not need him. I told myself the hollow could be filled.

And then he appeared again.

No warning. Just the sound of his bike in the distance, echoing over the fields, familiar and devastating.

By the time I opened the door, he was already standing there. Eyes on me.

We did not say hello. We did not need to. Because we both felt it immediately. The shift. The change. The ticking clock we could finally hear, loud and steady.

The project was history. The excuses were gone. We had run out of reasons. Still, he stepped inside in his usual way, shoes off. Like nothing had changed. But everything had.

And when he kissed me this time, it was slower. Not softer, never softer. But deeper. Like he was trying to memorise me from the inside out.

We did not rush.

We did not tear at each other.

We moved like people who knew this might be the last time. Or close to it.

Later, on the couch, his hand resting on my thigh, I almost asked. Almost inquired again. What happens now?

But I could not.

Because we both already knew.

Not much.

Just this.

For as long as we could keep it.

And maybe that was all it was ever meant to be.

Chapter 30

THE LONGING

"It is in the leaving that we learn what we cannot leave behind."
— **Rainer Maria Rilke**

The waiting had evolved into something else.

A slow, silent hollowing.

I stopped counting the days. I stopped pretending I knew when, or if, I would see him again.

It was no surprise.

But that did not make it hurt less.

Some mornings, I woke already yearning. Not just for him, though always for him, but for the feeling he left behind. The aliveness. The song that lived in my bones. The sense that my skin belonged to someone else's hands.

But the villa felt like an echo. Everything gone except the space he left behind. A silence that pressed into my bones.

The rice fields stretched on as far as ever. The sunsets still spilled gold and blood across the sky. The breeze still lifted the edge of my dress and kissed the back of my neck. But none of it touched me the same way. Because beauty, without someone to share it with, starts to feel like a kind of cruelty.

I told myself to enjoy it anyway. To sink into the stillness. To love what I had built, even alone.

And I tried.

But every night, I lay in the wide, empty bed, hands resting on my belly, staring at the ceiling, replaying him. The weight of his body. The scrape of his stubble. The quiet way he said my name when he thought I was not listening.

I no longer knew what I was waiting for. I just knew I could not seem to stop.

Outside, the fields lay flattened, waiting for water.

Dry.

Brittle.

Holding their breath for the next beginning.

Just like me.

Chapter 31

THE GOODBYE

"And that is how we grow, when the one we love leaves, and we are forced to find our own way."
— RUMI

It was not a fight.

There was no betrayal.

No explosion.

Just... the end.

Everything was complete. A new project called him away to another island. And just like that, the spell broke, quietly, gently, as if it had never really belonged to us at all.

One morning, he did not come.

And then another.

And another after that.

And I realised, with a hollow kind of calm, that he would not. Not like before. Not with the same ease. Not with the same certainty.

The secret had run out of places to hide.

I sent him a message. Just something simple.

Thank you for everything. The house looks beautiful.

And he replied, *Anytime, Queen.*

As if that was enough.

As if we had not built an entire world between glances and stolen hours.

And maybe it had to be. Because what else could we do? Ask for more? Demand what was never ours to keep?

No.

We knew the rules.

We knew the limits.

We knew this was always going to be borrowed time.

And yet...

Even now, standing alone on the terrace, watching the light shift over the fields, I swear I can still feel him. In the air. In the walls. In the quiet spaces where the secret used to live.

I do not know what comes next. I do not know how to unlearn the craving. I do know that, for a little while, we had something perfect.

Something impossible.

Something ours.

And maybe, in the end, that is enough.

Epilogue

WHAT STAYS

"And so it is, that love returns to the earth,
to grow again."
— UNKNOWN

Time passed. It always does.

The rains came again. Filling the paddies. Turning dust to mirror. The pause before the plough.

Shoots followed. Green rising from ruin.

And me? I stayed. Waiting to see what would grow next. Or if I still wanted to sow anything at all. Creating my space in the villa we built. In the life I made.

Some mornings, I still catch myself listening for the sound of his bike on the road. Long after, I know better. Long after, the messages have stopped.

I tell myself I should be over it by now. It was just a moment. A secret. A beautiful, impossible interlude.

But that is not the truth.

The truth is, some people become part of you. The way heat soaks into stone. The way a scent lingers on skin long after the source is gone. The way a glance across a half-finished room can rewrite your whole body.

I see him everywhere. Not literally. Not anymore. But in the way the light hits the floor at dusk. In the soft clink of coffee mugs on the counter.

In the way the breeze moves through the open doors. I half-expect to feel his hand on my back, guiding me forward.

It is quieter now. Lonelier, maybe. But it is also sweeter. Because I got to have it. We got to have it. And no one can take that.

It was ours. Still is, in some small way.

A secret I carry behind my heart.

A hum beneath the noise.

Forever.

Desire moves easily when it carries a foreign passport. That is the part no one tells you. You take what you want.

And you go.

The land stays.

The men stay.

The women, too.

And what you leave behind... sometimes that is the real story.

My bags were packed. The villa rented out. My last night in this dream. The hardest part complete.

The sun sank behind the fields, relieved, maybe, that I had finally stopped waiting.

And then I heard it. That low, familiar growl of a bike pulling into my driveway.

I did not move.

I did not rush to the door.

I just sat very still.

And listened.

It could be anyone. Of course, it could.

And yet.

As the engine cut out, as footsteps came nearer, I closed my eyes. And let myself believe, for just one more second, that maybe…

Maybe.

This was not over.

The footsteps stopped.

Close. Too close.

The door pushed open.

His eyes found mine, asking a thousand questions, pleading a thousand apologies.

And without a word, he placed something on the table.

A small offering. A sign. Mine to accept. Or not.

And then he waited.

For me to decide what came next.

The End

ABOUT THE AUTHOR

Alex Florschutz is a British writer, artist, and accidental collector of impossible love stories.

Her creative practice explores the power of transformation across various forms, including visual art, embodied psychology, sensual fiction, and soul storytelling.

She invites us to reclaim love, desire, and pleasure as pathways back to the truth of who we are.

Mad Enough to Love You: Desire is her debut work of fiction.

She lives in Bali, where the sunsets stretch longer than they should, and the past drifts like smoke, always close, never quite gone.

www.florschutz.com

"I will find you in every lifetime."
— Atticus